Dil, ~~Dosti,~~ Yaari

(A Tale of Friendship, Struggle & redemption)

By Raza Khatib

Copyright ©Raza khatib , 2024

All rights reserved. No part of this publication may be reproduced, stored in a retrieval system,or transmitted in any form or by any means, electronic, mechanical, recording or otherwise, without the prior written permission of the author.

This book has been published with all reasonable efforts taken to make the material error-free after the consent of the author. The author of this book is solely responsible and liable for its content including but not limited to the views, representations, descriptions, statements,

information, opinions and references ["Content"].

The publisher does not endorse or approve the Content of this book or guarantee the reliability,accuracy or completeness of the Content published herein. The publisher and the author all rights remains with the author and author only no copy should be re made or produced without the prior approval of author.make no representations or warranties of anykind with respect to this book or its contents. The author and the publisher disclaim all such representations and warranties, including for example warranties of merchantability and educational or medical advice for a particular purpose. In addition, the author and the publisher do not represent or warrant that the information accessible via this book is accurate, complete or current. We value our readers sISBN: xxxxxxxxxxxxx

Price ₹xxx

First Published in June, 2024.

Note:- The language used in this book is very simple so that every reader can have a great experience of reading,

Chapter 1: Gauravpur Ki Yaadein - Memories of Gauravpur

Gauravpur a quaint village nestled amidst lush green fields and rolling hills. It was a place where traditions held strong and the pace of life was slow and steady. Here, the mornings were greeted with the melodious chirping of birds and the aroma of fresh dew on the grass, while evenings were spent under the shimmering stars, with the village's age-old tales echoing through the air. The village was a tapestry of simple joys and profound connections, a place where every sunrise brought new possibilities and every sunset was a moment to reflect on the day's blessings.

In the heart of Gauravpur lived four inseparable friends: Aarav, Rajat, Rohan, and Vikram. They were a group as tight-knit as the threads in a family quilt, bound by their shared experiences and dreams. Their friendship had its roots in their earliest memories, growing stronger with each passing day. From childhood antics to adolescent dreams, their bond was a testament to the enduring power of camaraderie.

Aarav, the dreamer, had a poetic soul. His thoughts often wandered beyond the fields of Gauravpur, imagining worlds filled with endless possibilities. His fascination with the stars and the universe often led him to dream about places far beyond the village. His mother often found him lying on the grass, staring at the sky, lost in thought. Aarav's sketches of far-off places and fantastical creatures filled his notebook, each drawing a testament to his boundless imagination.

Rajat, the practical one, was known for his sharp mind and logical approach. He was the planner of the group, always thinking two steps ahead. Rajat's meticulous nature made him the unofficial leader when it came to organizing their adventures. Whether it was a simple trip to the river or a plan to build a treehouse, Rajat's strategic thinking ensured that everything went smoothly. His father, a farmer, often said that Rajat's mind was as fertile as the fields they ploughed.

Rohan, with his infectious laughter and boundless energy, brought joy to every moment. His enthusiasm was a constant source of motivation for his friends. Rohan's laughter was the soundtrack of their adventures, his jokes and stories lifting their spirits even in the toughest times. Known as the "firecracker" of the group, Rohan had a knack for turning the mundane into the extraordinary. His ability to find joy in the smallest things made him a beloved figure not just among his friends, but in the entire village.

Vikram, the quiet and introspective one, had a deep sense of loyalty and wisdom that belied his years. His reflective nature often led him to be the peacemaker in the group. Vikram's calm demeanour was a balm to his friends' fiery spirits. He had an innate understanding of people's emotions and was always the first to offer a comforting word or a shoulder to cry on. Vikram's wisdom often left the village elders nodding in approval, remarking that he was an old soul in a young body.

The four friends spent their days flying kites in the wide-open fields, their laughter mingling with the wind as their colourful kites soared high. The kite flying competitions were a highlight of their childhood, each boy determined to prove his kite-flying prowess. They raced their bicycles along the dusty village roads, feeling the thrill of freedom in the warm breeze against their faces. The bicycles, often hand-me-downs from older siblings, were their prized possessions, symbols of their growing independence. Under the ancient banyan tree, they studied together, helping each other with their lessons and sharing their dreams of a brighter future.

The banyan tree was more than just a study spot; it was a silent witness to their growth. Its sprawling branches provided shade during the hot summer days, and its roots were the perfect spot for their secret meetings. The tree was their confidante, its leaves rustling in agreement as they shared their deepest secrets and wildest dreams. On many occasions, they carved their initials into the tree's bark, a testament to their unbreakable bond.

Gauravpur was their playground and their sanctuary. The village festivals were a time of joy and celebration, where they participated in traditional dances, sang folk songs, and indulged in the delicious local delicacies. The annual harvest festival was their favourite, a time when the entire village came alive with colours, music, and laughter. The friends eagerly awaited the festival each year, participating in the various competitions and enjoying the festive foods prepared by their families. The river that flowed nearby was their escape during the hot summer days, its cool waters offering a refreshing respite. The river was their playground, its banks the site of many impromptu picnics and fishing expeditions.

Their bond was more than just friendship; it was a brotherhood. They stood by each other through thick and thin, their loyalty unwavering. They shared their deepest secrets, their hopes, and their fears. Each had a unique role within the group, and together, they were unstoppable. Aarav's dreams, Rajat's plans, Rohan's joy, and Vikram's wisdom created a synergy that was the heart of their friendship.

As they grew older, their dreams began to take shape. The horizon of Gauravpur no longer seemed sufficient to contain their aspirations. They yearned for more – more opportunities, more experiences, and a chance to make their mark on the world. The city of Mumbai, with its promise of endless possibilities, beckoned to them like a distant star. The stories of relatives who had moved to the city and achieved success filled their hearts with hope and ambition.

The decision to leave Gauravpur was not easy. It was a place that held all their childhood memories, their families, and the essence of who they were. They spent countless nights discussing their plans, weighing the pros and cons of leaving the only home they had ever known. The village elders, while supportive, reminded them of the challenges that lay ahead. The friends understood the enormity of the decision, but their desire to explore the world beyond Gauravpur was too strong to ignore.

Aarav was excited about the prospect of studying literature in Mumbai, envisioning a future where his stories could inspire others. Rajat dreamed of becoming an engineer, his plans meticulously laid out. Rohan, ever the entertainer, saw himself working in the bustling world of media and entertainment. Vikram, with his quiet determination, aimed to make a difference in the field of social work. Each of them had a unique dream, but they were united in their determination to succeed.

As the day of their departure approached, the village of Gauravpur rallied around them. Their families, friends, and neighbours came together to give them a heartfelt send-off. The village elders offered their blessings, while the younger children looked up to them with admiration and hope. The day before they left, the entire village gathered for a farewell feast, a celebration of their journey and the bonds that tied them to Gauravpur.

The morning of their departure was filled with a mix of excitement and melancholy. They hugged their families tightly, promising to make them proud. Aarav's mother handed him a small bag filled with homemade sweets, her eyes brimming with tears. Rajat's father gave him a firm handshake and a look of pride. Rohan's younger siblings clung to him, not wanting to let go. Vikram's grandmother pressed a small talisman into his hand, a symbol of protection.

As they boarded the train to Mumbai, they looked back at Gauravpur one last time. The fields, the river, the banyan tree – all the familiar sights that had shaped their lives. The train slowly pulled away from the station, and the village of Gauravpur began to recede into the distance. Their hearts were heavy, but their spirits were high. They were embarking on a new journey, one that would test their friendship and their resolve.

The journey to Mumbai was filled with anticipation and excitement. They watched the countryside whiz by, their minds filled with thoughts of the adventures that awaited them. They talked about their plans, their hopes, and their fears. Each one of them had a different dream, but they were united in their goal of making it big in the city.

Upon arriving in Mumbai, they were greeted by the cacophony of the bustling city. The towering skyscrapers, the throngs of people, and the constant hum of activity were a stark contrast to the serene life of Gauravpur. The city was overwhelming, its sheer size and pace unlike anything they had ever experienced. But they were not daunted. With the map of their dreams in their minds and the compass of friendship in their hearts, they set out to carve a path for themselves.

The initial days were tough. Finding a place to stay, adjusting to the fast-paced life, and securing jobs were challenges they faced head-on. They lived in a small, cramped apartment, but it was their haven. Late at night, they would sit on the terrace, looking out at the city lights, sharing their experiences and supporting each other. The city's challenges only strengthened their bond, each friend relying on the others to navigate the complexities of urban life.

Aarav found a job at a local publishing house, where he could nurture his love for writing. He spent his days surrounded by books, drawing inspiration from the literary world around him. Rajat joined a financial firm, utilizing his analytical skills. His ability to solve complex problems quickly earned him respect in his workplace. Rohan's charismatic personality landed him a position in a marketing agency, where his creativity shone through. Vikram started working at a tech company, his quiet determination making him an asset. His colleagues were impressed by his work ethic and dedication.

Despite the struggles, they never lost sight of their dreams or their bond. They celebrated each other's successes and provided a shoulder to lean on during tough times. Their friendship, which had been their strength in Gauravpur, continued to be their anchor in Mumbai. They explored the city together, finding joy in its diversity and vibrancy. From street food to cultural festivals, they embraced everything the city had to offer.

Together, they navigated the challenges of the city, learning and growing along the way. Their journey was just beginning, and with each step, they moved closer to their dreams, united by the memories of Gauravpur and the promise of a brighter future. The city of Mumbai, with its endless possibilities, was now their playground. Their bond, forged in the fields of Gauravpur, was the foundation on which they would build their future.

As they stood on the terrace of their apartment one evening, looking out at the city lights, they knew that their journey was just beginning. They had come a long way from the dusty roads and green fields of Gauravpur, but their friendship remained as strong as ever. With the stars above them and the city below, they felt a sense of limitless possibility. They were ready to take on the world, their hearts filled with hope and their spirits unbreakable.

In the heart of Mumbai, four friends from a small village stood united, their dreams intertwined, their destinies linked by the unbreakable bond of friendship. And as they looked ahead, they knew that no matter where life took them, the memories of Gauravpur would always be a guiding light, a reminder of where they came from and the dreams that had brought them together.

Chapter 2: Safar Ki Shuruaat - The Beginning of the Journey

With stars in their eyes and determination in their hearts, Aarav, Rajat, Rohan, and Vikram bid farewell to their beloved village and set out for the city of dreams - Mumbai. They were armed with nothing but their aspirations and the unwavering bond of friendship that bound them together. This chapter explores their final days in Gauravpur, the emotional goodbyes, and the exciting yet daunting journey to Mumbai.

Gauravpur's Last Glance

As the departure day loomed closer, the four friends spent every remaining moment soaking in the essence of Gauravpur. Each corner of the village held a memory, each street a story. They revisited the banyan tree where they had spent countless hours discussing dreams and sharing secrets. Aarav took one last sketch of the landscape, hoping to capture the serenity of the village in his notebook. Rajat meticulously noted every detail of their journey, ensuring nothing was left to chance. Rohan organized a small farewell gathering for their close friends and families, and Vikram penned down his thoughts, intending to write a reflective piece on their transition from village life to city aspirations.

The evening before their departure was filled with mixed emotions. Their families gathered to bid them farewell. Aarav's mother prepared his favourite dishes, trying to mask her anxiety with a smile. Rajat's father handed him a leather-bound diary, symbolizing the next chapter of his life. Rohan's siblings, teary-eyed, clung to him, making him promise to return soon. Vikram's grandmother, with wisdom in her eyes, gave him a handcrafted talisman for protection.

The village elders, respected figures in Gauravpur, gave their blessings, reminding the friends to stay true to their roots. The villagers, who had watched them grow up, offered words of encouragement and pride. As the night drew to a close, the friends sat around a bonfire, reminiscing about their childhood adventures, laughing and crying, aware that the dawn would bring a new beginning.

The Journey Begins

On the morning of their departure, the village gathered at the train station. The platform buzzed with a mix of excitement and sorrow. The train, a symbol of their transition, stood ready to take them to Mumbai. As they boarded, they turned back to wave at the familiar faces, the people who had shaped their lives. The train whistle blew, and with a chugging start, their journey began.

The journey to Mumbai was a blend of anticipation and contemplation. The countryside whizzed by, a blur of green fields and small towns, each mile bringing them closer to their dreams. Aarav immersed himself in writing, jotting down his thoughts and emotions. Rajat studied the city map and planned their first few days. Rohan entertained fellow passengers with his stories, making the long journey feel shorter. Vikram, with his journal in hand, captured the essence of the transition, noting every significant moment.

As the train approached Mumbai, the landscape began to change. The vast fields gave way to concrete structures, and the air buzzed with the energy of the city. They were both nervous and excited, aware that Mumbai was a world apart from the tranquil life of Gauravpur. They held onto each other, finding strength in their unity, ready to face the unknown challenges of the city.

Chapter 3: Duniya Ka Rang – The Colours of the World

Mumbai welcomed them with open arms, offering a kaleidoscope of opportunities and challenges. This chapter delves into their initial experiences in the city, their individual journeys, and how their friendship continued to be their guiding light amidst the hustle and bustle of Mumbai.

Mumbai: The First Impression

Stepping onto the platform at Mumbai Central, the friends were hit by a wave of new sensations. The noise, the crowd, the sheer scale of the city was overwhelming. Skyscrapers loomed in the distance, and the streets were a maze of activity. They navigated through the crowd, clutching their bags and hopes tightly.

Their first challenge was finding accommodation. Mumbai's real estate was notorious for being expensive and scarce. After a tiring day of searching, they found a small apartment in a bustling neighbourhood. It was cramped and far from luxurious, but it was their new home. The friends spent the first night unpacking and setting up their space, their spirits high despite the modest conditions. They decorated the apartment with mementos from Gauravpur, ensuring that their new home had a piece of their old one.

Aarav's Journey: The World of Software

Aarav, the dreamer with a poetic soul, found his place in the world of software. He had always been fascinated by technology and its potential to create and inspire. His job at a local software company allowed him to combine his creative thinking with technical skills. The initial days were challenging; the pace was fast, and the expectations were high. Aarav spent long hours coding and learning, often staying up late to perfect his projects. His creativity shone through in his work, earning him the admiration of his colleagues. Despite the pressure, Aarav found solace in the creative aspects of his job. He often spent his evenings on the terrace, sketching the cityscape, finding parallels between the complexity of the city and the intricacies of his code.

Rajat's Journey: The Entrepreneur

Rajat, the practical planner, ventured into entrepreneurship. He had always been fascinated by the idea of building something from the ground up. He joined a start-up incubator, surrounded by like-minded individuals driven by ambition and innovation. Rajat's logical approach and strategic thinking were invaluable as he navigated the challenges of the start-up world. He worked tirelessly, often skipping meals and sleep, focused on turning ideas into reality. Rajat's start-up, a tech solution for small businesses, started gaining traction. He faced numerous hurdles – funding issues, market competition, and technical glitches – but his perseverance paid off. Rajat's disciplined approach and ability to foresee potential problems helped his start-up survive the critical early stages.

Rohan's Journey: The Marketer

Rohan, with his infectious energy and charisma, embraced the realm of marketing. His job at a leading marketing agency was a perfect fit for his outgoing personality. Rohan's ability to connect with people and his creative flair made him a star in his field. He was quickly noticed for his innovative campaign ideas and his knack for understanding consumer behaviour. Rohan's days were filled with meetings, brainstorming sessions, and client interactions. He thrived in the dynamic environment, his enthusiasm contagious. Despite the demanding schedule, Rohan ensured he stayed connected with his friends, often organizing weekend outings to explore the city and unwind from the hectic work week.

Vikram's Journey: The Journalist

Vikram, the quiet and introspective one, found his calling in journalism. His passion for stories and understanding of human nature made him a natural fit for the profession. He joined a renowned newspaper, starting as a junior reporter. Vikram's assignments took him across the city, covering a wide range of stories – from political events to human interest pieces. His empathetic approach and attention to detail made his articles stand out. Vikram's work was demanding, often requiring him to work odd hours and meet tight deadlines. However, he found fulfilment in giving voice to the unheard and bringing important issues to light. Vikram's experiences as a journalist broadened his perspective, deepening his understanding of the complexities of urban life.

Navigating Challenges Together

The path to success was fraught with obstacles. Each friend faced unique challenges in their respective fields. Aarav struggled with the pressure of deadlines and the need to constantly innovate. Rajat dealt with the uncertainty of the start-up world, where success was never guaranteed. Rohan faced fierce competition in the marketing industry, requiring him to continuously prove his worth. Vikram encountered the harsh realities of journalism, where the pursuit of truth often came at a personal cost.

Yet, with each hurdle they overcame, their friendship grew stronger. The evenings were their time to unwind and recharge. They would gather in their small apartment, sharing stories of their day, offering advice and support. Aarav's sketches, Rajat's strategic insights, Rohan's humour, and Vikram's reflective thoughts created a balanced environment. Their apartment became a sanctuary, a place where they could be themselves without any pretences.

On weekends, they explored Mumbai together, experiencing the city's rich culture and diversity. They visited historical sites, enjoyed street food, and attended cultural festivals. These outings were a reminder of their shared dreams and the journey they were on together. The city's vibrancy and energy mirrored their ambitions, fuelling their determination to succeed.

Celebrating Successes and Learning from Failures

Their journey was marked by both successes and failures. Aarav's first software release was a significant milestone, a testament to his hard work and creativity. Rajat's start-up secured its first major client, a moment of validation for his entrepreneurial spirit. Rohan's marketing campaign won an industry award, recognizing his innovative approach. Vikram's investigative article uncovered a major scandal, earning him accolades and respect in the journalism community.

However, there were also moments of failure and disappointment. Aarav faced criticism for a project that didn't meet expectations. Rajat's start-up experienced a financial setback, threatening its survival. Rohan lost a major client to a competitor, a blow to his confidence. Vikram's article on a sensitive topic led to backlash, testing his resolve. Each failure was a learning experience, a step towards growth and improvement.

Their friendship was their anchor during these times. They celebrated each other's successes with genuine joy and supported each other through failures with unwavering solidarity. The bond they had forged in Gauravpur proved to be their greatest strength in Mumbai. It was a reminder of their roots and the dreams that had brought them together.

Chapter 4: Mohabbat Ka Safar - Journey of Love

Aarav's Encounter with Priya

Amidst the hustle and bustle of Mumbai, where dreams and ambitions collided in a cacophony of aspirations, Aarav stumbled upon a serene oasis that would change his life forever. It was a typical morning, the city already alive with the frenetic energy of commuters and vendors setting up their stalls. Aarav, lost in thought as he navigated the crowded streets, caught a whiff of freshly brewed coffee that beckoned him towards a small, unassuming café tucked away from the chaos.

The café, with its cosy interior and the aroma of coffee mingling with soft music, offered a stark contrast to the bustling streets outside. Aarav found himself drawn to a corner table, where he settled with his laptop, seeking a moment of respite from the rush. It was here that his eyes met Priya's for the first time.

Priya, behind the counter, exuded a quiet elegance and warmth that instantly captivated Aarav. She had an air of serenity amidst the morning rush, a gentle smile playing on her lips as she took orders and engaged in brief exchanges with customers. Aarav found himself stealing glances, drawn not just by her physical beauty but by the palpable sense of peace she seemed to carry with her.

Over the next few weeks, Aarav became a regular at the café, his visits no longer just about coffee and a quiet workspace. Each encounter with Priya deepened their connection, their conversations evolving from polite exchanges to heartfelt dialogues about art, life, and their shared passions. Aarav discovered that Priya was not just a café attendant; she was an artist whose paintings adorned the café walls, each piece reflecting her soulful perspective on life.

The Blossoming of Love

Aarav and Priya's relationship blossomed against the vibrant tapestry of Mumbai's cultural and artistic landscape. They spent their days exploring the city's hidden gems – art galleries showcasing avant-garde exhibits, poetry readings in dimly lit cafés where the spoken word resonated with emotion, and lazy afternoons by the Arabian Sea, watching the waves kiss the shore under the warmth of the sun.

Priya's presence became a calming influence in Aarav's life, a counterbalance to the relentless pace of his professional ambitions. As Aarav delved deeper into his work in software development, experimenting with ideas that merged technology with his poetic sensibilities, Priya stood by him with unwavering support. She encouraged his creativity, offering insights and perspectives that enriched his projects.

Their evenings were filled with laughter and shared dreams. They strolled through Mumbai's bustling markets, sampling street food delicacies that teased their taste buds.

At night, they gazed at the city lights from Marine Drive, finding solace in each other's company amidst the chaos of urban life.

Aarav and Priya's Journey Together

As their love deepened, Aarav and Priya began to weave their individual aspirations into a shared tapestry of dreams. Priya, emboldened by Aarav's belief in her artistic talent, found the courage to exhibit her paintings in local galleries. Aarav, fuelled by Priya's encouragement and the depth of their connection, poured his heart into a personal project – a software application designed not just for functionality but as a medium of artistic expression.

Their journey together was marked by milestones both personal and professional. Aarav's project garnered attention for its innovative approach, blending cutting-edge technology with intuitive design inspired by Priya's art. Priya, in turn, received accolades for her paintings, which captured the essence of Mumbai's soul through vibrant colours and emotive brushstrokes.

Their friends – Rajat, Rohan, and Vikram – witnessed the transformation in Aarav with a mixture of joy and admiration. They welcomed Priya into their close-knit circle, recognizing the positive impact she had on Aarav's life. Priya's warmth and kindness endeared her to them, and she became an integral part of their lives, attending gatherings where her presence added a new dimension of harmony and camaraderie.

The Depth of Their Connection

At the heart of Aarav and Priya's relationship was a deep emotional connection forged through shared experiences and mutual understanding. They navigated the challenges of their respective careers with resilience, drawing strength from each other's unwavering support. Aarav found in Priya a partner who believed in his dreams as passionately as he did, while Priya discovered in Aarav a soulmate who cherished her creativity and nurtured her artistic journey.

Their bond was not without its challenges. The demands of their careers often tested their commitment to each other, requiring them to strike a delicate balance between professional ambitions and personal fulfilment. There were moments of doubt and uncertainty, conflicts that arose from differing priorities, yet their love remained steadfast, a beacon of hope and stability amidst the ebb and flow of urban life.

The Proposal

As their relationship reached a pivotal moment, Aarav knew that Priya was the one he wanted to spend his life with. He meticulously planned a proposal that would be as memorable as their journey together. It was an evening at the café where they had first met, transformed into a romantic haven adorned with fairy lights and Priya's paintings, each canvas a testament to their shared memories and aspirations.

With nerves tingling and heart racing, Aarav knelt before Priya, his eyes filled with love and determination. He poured his heart out, expressing his deepest feelings and his unwavering commitment to their future together. Priya, overwhelmed with emotion and joy, accepted his proposal with tears of happiness, sealing their love with a promise to cherish and support each other through all the chapters yet to come.

Their engagement was a celebration not just of their love but of the journey that had brought them together – a journey marked by serendipity, shared dreams, and the transformative power of love amidst the chaos of Mumbai.

Chapter 5: Dosti Ki Parakh – Test of Friendship

Vikram's Temptation

In the sprawling metropolis of Mumbai, where dreams glittered like city lights and ambitions soared amidst skyscrapers, Vikram's journey took an unexpected turn. Success in journalism had swiftly opened doors to a world of possibilities, but it also introduced him to temptations that tested the very foundation of his friendships.

The allure of Mumbai's nightlife beckoned like a siren's call – a world of glamour, luxury, and easy money that seemed worlds away from the simplicity of Gauravpur and the earnest dreams they once shared under the shade of the banyan tree. Vikram found himself drawn into this glittering facade, where prestige and pleasure intermingled under the city's neon glow.

At first, it was innocent curiosity that led Vikram to attend exclusive parties and events frequented by the city's elite. The thrill of rubbing shoulders with influential personalities and celebrities fuelled his ambition, offering a tantalizing glimpse into a life beyond the confines of routine journalism. Yet, beneath the surface allure lay a darker undercurrent that would soon pull Vikram into its depths.

The Drift

As Vikram's forays into Mumbai's nightlife increased, his presence among his friends – Aarav, Rajat, and Rohan – became sporadic. The once inseparable quartet, bound by childhood memories and shared aspirations, began to feel the strain of Vikram's newfound lifestyle. Rajat, the pragmatic planner of the group, noticed the subtle changes first – missed gatherings, delayed responses, and a growing disconnect that hinted at deeper issues.

Rohan, the lively spirit whose infectious laughter had always been a beacon of camaraderie, attempted to organize outings and reunions to reignite the bond they had cherished for so long. Aarav, navigating the delicate balance between his blossoming relationship with Priya and the demands of his career, struggled to bridge the growing gap with Vikram, who seemed increasingly distant.

Confrontation and Realization

The tension came to a head one fateful night, orchestrated by Rohan in a bid to reclaim the camaraderie that had defined their friendship. Vikram's arrival, however, marked a turning point tinged with confrontation and confrontation. In a state fuelled by alcohol and the intoxicating allure of the nightlife, Vikram unleashed a torrent of pent-up emotions, accusing his friends of failing to understand his new life and dismissing their concerns with reckless abandon.

Aarav, stunned and hurt by Vikram's words, found himself grappling with conflicting emotions – the loyalty to a friendship forged in the innocence of childhood and the bitter sting of betrayal. Rajat, typically composed and rational, articulated the collective disappointment, outlining the changes that had strained their once unbreakable bond. Rohan, the heart of their group, pleaded for reconciliation, his voice tinged with sadness at the fractures that had marred their unity.

A Moment of Crisis

In the aftermath of the confrontation, the group found itself adrift in a sea of uncertainty. The rift caused by Vikram's actions cast a shadow over their shared memories and dreams. Days turned into weeks as Rajat, Rohan, and Aarav grappled with the fallout, their efforts to reach out to Vikram met with silence or half-hearted responses that only deepened the wounds.

Aarav, torn between his loyalty to Vikram and the burgeoning relationship with Priya, found solace in her unwavering support. Priya, with her empathetic nature and deep understanding of human emotions, offered

Aarav a sanctuary amidst the turmoil. Together, they navigated the emotional landscape, confronting the complexities of friendship and betrayal.

Vikram, meanwhile, faced his own reckoning in the solitude of introspection. The superficial allure of the nightlife began to lose its lustre, revealing the hollow emptiness beneath the surface glamour. Alone with his thoughts, he grappled with the consequences of his choices – the friendships fractured, the dreams deferred, and the undeniable truth of his own vulnerability.

The Path to Redemption

Vikram's journey to redemption was arduous and fraught with challenges, requiring him to confront his inner demons and make difficult choices. He decided to step away from his demanding job and the allure of Mumbai's nightlife, retreating to the familiar embrace of Gauravpur. Amidst the tranquil simplicity of village life, surrounded by the echoes of childhood memories, Vikram sought clarity and resolution.

In the quietude of Gauravpur, far removed from the hustle of Mumbai, Vikram rediscovered the essence of his roots. The verdant fields and familiar faces offered him a sanctuary to reflect on the choices that had led him astray. He sought counsel from his family, drawing strength from their unconditional love and wisdom.

Rebuilding the Bond

With newfound resolve, Vikram returned to Mumbai, determined to mend the fractures he had caused. He reached out to Aarav, Rajat, and Rohan, bearing his soul with humility and remorse. The reunion was fraught with emotions – tears shed, apologies offered, and wounds slowly healed. Aarav, torn between forgiveness and lingering hurt, found himself grappling with the complexity of rebuilding trust.

Rajat, pragmatic as ever, outlined the conditions for reconciliation – a commitment to honesty, mutual respect, and shared aspirations. Rohan, the optimist whose infectious spirit had weathered many storms, extended a hand of friendship, eager to restore the bonds that had once defined their unity.

Aarav and Priya's Role

Throughout Vikram's journey of redemption, Aarav found solace and strength in Priya's unwavering support. Her empathetic understanding of human emotions and the complexities of relationships provided Aarav with a sanctuary amidst the turmoil. Together, they navigated the emotional landscape, confronting the intricacies of friendship and betrayal with courage and resilience.

Priya's presence brought a sense of balance and harmony to the group. Her kindness and empathy helped heal the wounds that had threatened to sever their bonds, creating an environment where forgiveness and understanding could flourish. As Aarav and Priya navigated the challenges of their own relationship, their love became a guiding light for Vikram, illuminating the path to redemption and renewal.

The Healing Process

The healing process was gradual yet transformative, marked by moments of reflection, reconciliation, and renewal. Vikram, humbled by the forgiveness of his friends and the depth of their enduring bond, committed himself to rebuilding what had been lost. He embraced change, distancing himself from the toxic influences that had led him astray, and prioritizing the friendships that had stood the test of time.

Together, Aarav, Rajat, Rohan, and Vikram revisited their old haunts and created new memories that celebrated their shared history and the resilience of their friendship. They navigated the complexities of adulthood with a renewed sense of unity, drawing strength from their collective experiences and the unwavering support of loved ones.

Chapter 6: Darr Se Jung - Battle Against Fear

Vikram's Descent

Mumbai, the city of dreams, shimmered with promise under the neon lights that adorned its skyline. For Vikram, a young journalist whose career had soared to unforeseen heights, Mumbai offered not just opportunities but also temptations. The initial allure of prestige and pleasure soon gave way to a darker reality as Vikram found himself ensnared in the web of Mumbai's nightlife.

The nights in Mumbai blurred into days, each moment consumed by the hollow promises of excess and indulgence. What started as networking events and celebrations of professional milestones gradually morphed into a relentless pursuit of escapism. Alcohol flowed freely, its intoxicating embrace offering temporary respite from the pressures of Vikram's demanding job and the weight of personal insecurities.

Signs of Strain

Amidst the glittering facade of success, cracks began to appear in the foundation of Vikram's life – signs that were not lost on his closest friends, Aarav, Rajat, and Rohan. Aarav, the introspective dreamer whose own journey had led him to discover love amidst the chaos of Mumbai, noticed the subtle shifts in Vikram's demeanour. The dark circles under his eyes spoke volumes of sleepless nights and the toll of excessive indulgence. Rajat, the pragmatic planner of their group, observed with growing concern the distant gaze that betrayed inner turmoil, a silent scream for help masked by a facade of bravado. Rohan, the spirited heart of their circle, tried to organize gatherings in futile attempts to rekindle the camaraderie they once cherished, sensing the impending storm but unsure how to weather it.

Intervention and Resistance

The turning point arrived amidst a haze of alcohol and fractured memories, a night when the boundaries between celebration and self-destruction blurred into insignificance. Aarav, torn between his unwavering loyalty to Vikram and the newfound stability of his relationship with Priya, found himself at a crossroads of emotions. With Priya's steadfast support, he summoned the courage to confront Vikram with empathy and resolve, urging him to confront the destructive path that threatened to unravel the fabric of their friendship. Rajat, the voice of reason hardened by the stark realities of adulthood, outlined the stark consequences of Vikram's actions – shattered dreams, fractured bonds, and the looming spectre of addiction that cast a long shadow over their shared aspirations.

Vikram's Breaking Point

In a rare moment of clarity amidst the chaos that had become his life, Vikram confronted his inner demons with a courage born of desperation. The once-enticing allure of Mumbai's nightlife, with its promises of belonging and liberation, now revealed its true face – a relentless cycle of emptiness and despair. Alone with his thoughts, he grappled with the weight of his choices – friendships strained to the breaking point, dreams deferred in favour of temporary pleasures, and the undeniable truth of his own vulnerability laid bare before him.

The breaking point was not just a culmination of external pressures but an internal reckoning with the consequences of his actions. The friendships that had once been his anchor now seemed frayed, their bonds stretched thin by the demands of his escalating addiction. The dreams they had once shared – of conquering Mumbai's vibrant landscape, of leaving a mark on the world through their respective passions – now hung in the balance, threatened by the reckless abandon that had become Vikram's coping mechanism.

Exploring the Depths

To truly understand Vikram's descent, we must delve into the labyrinthine corridors of his mind, where shadows danced with memories of past successes and future uncertainties. The allure of Mumbai's nightlife, with its promise of belonging and escape, became a siren song that Vikram could not resist. Each night out was a gamble, a temporary reprieve from the pressures of deadlines and expectations that awaited him at the office. The pulse of the city, amplified by the thumping beats of nightclubs and the laughter of revellers, offered a fleeting sense of freedom that Vikram craved in moments of vulnerability.

Yet, beneath the surface glitter, lay a darker truth – the toll that addiction took on Vikram's mental and emotional well-being. The initial thrill of stepping into exclusive venues and rubbing shoulders with the city's elite gave way to a gnawing emptiness, a void that no amount of alcohol or companionship could fill. The friendships that had once anchored him now felt like distant memories, their absence a stark reminder of the rift that had widened between Vikram and his closest confidants.

Intervention and Resistance

The signs of strain were evident to those who knew Vikram best. Aarav, Rajat, and Rohan, united by bonds forged in the innocence of youth and strengthened through shared dreams, watched with growing concern as their friend spiralled deeper into the abyss of addiction. Aarav, whose own journey had led him to find love amidst the chaos of Mumbai, struggled to reconcile his loyalty to Vikram with the stability that Priya offered him. Her unwavering support became a lifeline as he navigated the complexities of confronting a friend in crisis, her presence a source of strength and clarity in moments of doubt.

Rajat, the pragmatic planner whose sharp intellect had guided their group through countless challenges, recognized the signs of Vikram's descent with a sobering clarity. The dark circles under his eyes, the erratic behaviour that veered between moments of exuberance and despondency – each was a silent plea for intervention, a call to action that Rajat could not ignore. His attempts to reason with Vikram were met with resistance, a stubborn refusal to acknowledge the depth of his own vulnerability.

Rohan, the spirited heart of their circle whose infectious laughter had once been the glue that bound them together, found himself at a loss for words as he witnessed the unravelling of their once-unbreakable bond. His efforts to organize gatherings and rekindle the camaraderie they had cherished seemed futile in the face of Vikram's escalating addiction. Yet, beneath his outward optimism lay a deep-seated concern for a friend whose descent mirrored the city's relentless pursuit of glamour and excess.

Confrontation and Realization

The turning point came on a night tinged with the haze of alcohol and fractured memories, a night when emotions ran high and resolutions hung in the balance. Aarav, bolstered by Priya's unwavering support and the clarity that comes with confronting a friend in crisis, found himself at a crossroads of emotions. His plea for Vikram to confront the destructive path he had chosen was rooted in empathy and a shared history that transcended the challenges of adulthood.

Rajat, whose voice of reason had guided their group through countless challenges, outlined the stark consequences of Vikram's actions with a pragmatism born of necessity. The shattered dreams, the fractured bonds, and the looming spectre of addiction cast a long shadow over their shared aspirations, threatening to unravel the fabric of their friendship.

Yet, amidst the chaos that had become his life, Vikram found a rare moment of clarity – a reckoning with the consequences of his choices and the toll that addiction took on his mental and emotional well-being. The allure of Mumbai's nightlife, once a beacon of false promises, now revealed its true face – a relentless cycle of emptiness and despair that Vikram could no longer ignore.

Vikram's Breaking Point

In a moment of courage born of desperation, Vikram confronted his inner demons with a clarity that had eluded him in moments of vulnerability. The friendships that had once anchored him now seemed frayed, their bonds stretched thin by the demands of his escalating addiction. The dreams they had once shared – of conquering Mumbai's vibrant landscape, of leaving a mark on the world through their respective passions – now hung in the balance, threatened by the reckless abandon that had become Vikram's coping mechanism.

The breaking point was not just a culmination of external pressures but an internal reckoning with the consequences of his actions. The friendships that had once been his anchor now seemed frayed, their bonds stretched thin by the demands of his escalating addiction. The dreams they had once shared – of conquering Mumbai's vibrant landscape, of leaving a mark on the world through their respective passions – now hung in the balance, threatened by the reckless abandon that had become Vikram's coping mechanism.

Chapter 7: Umeed Ka Kiran - Ray of Hope

Journey of Recovery

With the unwavering support of his friends, Vikram embarked on the arduous journey of recovery. He sought solace in the tranquil embrace of Gauravpur, where the verdant fields and familiar faces offered a sanctuary for introspection and healing. Surrounded by the echoes of childhood memories, he sought counsel from his family, drawing strength from their unconditional love and wisdom.

Redemption and Reconciliation

Upon his return to Mumbai, Vikram confronted the wreckage of his past with humility and resolve. He reached out to Aarav, Rajat, and Rohan, bearing his soul with heartfelt apologies and a determination to mend the fractures he had caused. Their reunion was fraught with emotions – tears shed, forgiveness sought, and wounds slowly healed. Aarav, grappling with the complexity of rebuilding trust, found solace in Priya's unwavering support and the healing power of their love.

The Path Forward

Together, Aarav, Rajat, Rohan, and Vikram navigated the complexities of adulthood with a renewed sense of unity and purpose. They revisited old haunts and created new memories that celebrated their shared history and the resilience of their friendship. Vikram's journey of redemption became a testament to the transformative power of forgiveness and the enduring strength of human connection.

Chapter 8: Yaari Ka Safar - Journey of Friendship

Introduction

As the sun sets over the bustling city of Mumbai, casting its golden glow upon the towering skyscrapers and bustling streets, the essence of friendship illuminates the lives of four inseparable friends: Aarav, Rajat, Rohan, and Vikram. This chapter delves deep into their journey through adversity, exploring how their bond evolved and strengthened amidst the trials and tribulations they faced together. It's a tale of resilience, forgiveness, and the profound connection that binds them beyond mere friendship.

Setting the Stage

Mumbai, the city of dreams, had been both a crucible and a playground for Aarav, Rajat, Rohan, and Vikram. Each had arrived in the city with dreams as diverse as their personalities. For Aarav, it was a quest for creative fulfillment and love; Rajat sought entrepreneurial success; Rohan embraced the vibrant world of marketing, and Vikram initially found his calling in journalism. Amidst the towering skyscrapers and the chaotic streets, their paths intertwined, their shared experiences weaving a tapestry of camaraderie and mutual support.

Trials and Tribulations

Vikram's Struggle with Addiction

The journey of friendship took a tumultuous turn when Vikram, seduced by Mumbai's nightlife and the allure of success, fell into the abyss of addiction. His descent into self-destruction strained the bonds that had once seemed unbreakable. Aarav, Rajat, and Rohan, witnessing Vikram's struggle, were faced with their own tests of loyalty and understanding. They tried to intervene, to reason with him, to bring him back from the brink. Each encounter was fraught with emotion, with Vikram oscillating between moments of clarity and depths of despair.

Aarav's Balancing Act

For Aarav, navigating his burgeoning relationship with Priya while grappling with Vikram's crisis posed a delicate balancing act. Priya's unwavering support became a pillar of strength as Aarav sought to reconcile his loyalty to Vikram with the stability of his newfound love. Their journey together through Mumbai's cultural landscape, from art galleries to street markets, offered moments of solace amidst the chaos. Priya's presence brought a calming influence, reminding Aarav of the importance of empathy and patience in times of adversity.

Rajat's Pragmatic Approach

Rajat, the pragmatic planner of the group, faced Vikram's crisis with a sharp intellect and a sense of responsibility. He outlined the consequences of Vikram's actions, not just for himself but for their shared dreams and aspirations. His attempts to reason with Vikram were grounded in practicality, emphasizing the need for accountability and the importance of facing one's demons. Rajat's steadfastness became a guiding light for the group, offering clarity amidst the emotional turmoil that threatened to engulf them.

Rohan's Heartfelt Efforts

Meanwhile, Rohan, with his infectious laughter and boundless energy, tried to rekindle the camaraderie they had once cherished. He organized gatherings, encouraged shared experiences, and reminded Vikram of the joy they had found together in simpler times. Rohan's efforts were driven by a deep-seated belief in the power of friendship to overcome even the darkest of challenges. His optimism became a beacon of hope, reminding his friends of the resilience that lay within them.

Confrontation and Resolution

The Breaking Point

The turning point came one fateful night when Vikram, consumed by the throes of addiction, lashed out at his friends in a moment of despair. Emotions ran high as years of friendship hung in the balance. Aarav, torn between his loyalty to Vikram and the need to protect his own emotional well-being, found himself at a crossroads. Priya's presence offered him solace and clarity, grounding him in the strength of their love amidst the turmoil.

Vikram's Redemption

In a moment of clarity amidst the chaos, Vikram confronted his inner demons with a courage born of desperation. The superficial allure of Mumbai's nightlife faded, revealing its true face – a cycle of emptiness and despair that Vikram could no longer ignore. Alone with his thoughts, he grappled with the consequences of his choices – the fractured friendships, the deferred dreams, and the undeniable truth of his own vulnerability.

Rebuilding Trust and Friendship

Vikram's path to redemption was not easy. It required him to confront his demons, to seek help, and to make amends for the hurt he had caused. His decision to take a break from the city, to seek solace in the simplicity of his roots in Gauravpur, became a journey of self-discovery and renewal. Supported by his family and guided by the lessons learned from his friends, Vikram returned to Mumbai with a renewed sense of purpose.

Chapter 9: The Essence of Friendship

Unity in Diversity

Through their journey of adversity, Aarav, Rajat, Rohan, and Vikram discovered the true essence of friendship – a bond that transcended time and space, uniting them in heart, soul, and spirit. Their shared experiences, from the heights of success to the depths of despair, forged a connection that was stronger than ever before. They learned to lean on each other's strengths, to forgive each other's shortcomings, and to celebrate each other's victories as their own.

Lessons Learned

The journey of friendship taught them invaluable lessons about resilience, empathy, and the power of unconditional support. They learned that true friendship is not just about sharing moments of joy but also about weathering storms together, emerging stronger and more united than before. Each of them grew in their own way – Aarav found stability and love in Priya's embrace, Rajat honed his pragmatism into a tool for guidance, Rohan's optimism became a beacon of hope, and Vikram confronted his vulnerabilities with courage and humility.

Looking Ahead

As the sun sets on another day in Mumbai, casting its golden glow upon the world below, Aarav, Rajat, Rohan, and Vikram stand together, their bond unbreakable. They have faced the trials and tribulations of life with courage and resilience, emerging victorious in their battle against adversity. The city's skyline, once a backdrop to their individual struggles, now stands as a testament to their enduring friendship – a journey of love, loss, and redemption that has shaped their lives forever.

Chapter 10: Seeds of Envy - Jealousy Takes Root

Introduction

After Aarav's remarkable achievement in clearing the civil services examination and securing a prestigious position as an IAS officer, his friends Rajat and Rohan find themselves grappling with a whirlwind of emotions. While they genuinely celebrate Aarav's success, beneath the surface lies a complex mix of pride, admiration, and an unexpected undercurrent of jealousy and envy. This chapter delves into the intricate dynamics of their friendship as jealousy begins to take root, potentially straining the bonds forged through years of shared dreams and challenges in Mumbai.

Aarav's Triumph and the Ripple Effect

Aarav's journey to success had been a testament to perseverance, dedication, and the unwavering support of his friends. His achievement was not just a personal victory but a culmination of the dreams they had nurtured together since their days in Gauravpur. As news of Aarav's success spread through their circle, the initial reaction was one of genuine happiness and pride. They celebrated his accomplishment wholeheartedly, showering him with congratulations and admiration

Rajat's Perspective: The Pragmatic Planner

The Seeds of Envy

For Rajat, the news of Aarav's success stirred a complex maelstrom of emotions. As the pragmatic planner of their group, Rajat had always envisioned his own path to success, often revolving around entrepreneurial ventures and innovative business ideas. While he outwardly expressed joy for Aarav, internally, he couldn't escape the gnawing feeling of comparison. Envy planted seeds of doubt about his own journey and achievements, sparking a subtle conflict within.

Internal Conflict

Rajat's internal struggle stemmed from a deep-seated sense of inadequacy, juxtaposed against the pride he felt for Aarav. He wrestled with questions about his own choices and aspirations, contemplating whether he had chosen the right path or if there were missed opportunities along the way. The stark contrast between his pragmatic approach and the emotional turmoil of jealousy created a turbulent inner landscape, challenging his perception of success and friendship.

Navigating Friendship and Competition

As Rajat grappled with these conflicting emotions, he found himself subtly withdrawing from the celebratory atmosphere surrounding Aarav's achievement. While he maintained an outward facade of support, internally, he struggled to reconcile his genuine admiration for Aarav with the simmering envy that threatened to strain their friendship. Rajat sought solace in moments of introspection, reflecting deeply on the trajectory of his ambitions and the evolving dynamics of their close-knit group.

Rohan's Perspective: The Spirited Heart

The Challenge of Envy

Rohan, known for his vibrant spirit and unwavering energy, faced a different but equally profound challenge in the wake of Aarav's success. As someone who had carved out a niche in marketing through creativity and perseverance, Rohan had always thrived on challenges. However, Aarav's accomplishment triggered a wave of self-doubt. Despite his genuine happiness for Aarav, envy crept in, casting shadows over his own achievements and career choices. Rohan's journey through Mumbai had been a rollercoaster of highs and lows, driven by his passion for marketing and an unyielding pursuit of success. Aarav's success forced him to confront buried insecurities, stirring feelings of inadequacy about his own achievements. He questioned whether he had made the right career choices and if he could have accomplished more. The comparison to Aarav, whom he deeply admired, evoked a mix of respect and envy within him. Despite grappling with internal turmoil, Rohan remained a steadfast pillar of support for Aarav and their group. His outward demeanour remained positive and encouraging, masking the inner conflict he battled silently. He immersed himself in work and social activities, attempting to distract himself from the unsettling emotions threatening to disrupt the harmony of their friendship. His efforts to uphold a facade of optimism became both a shield and a burden as he navigated through uncharted emotional territory.

Aarav's Perspective: Balancing Triumph and Humility

Gratitude and Humility

Amidst the celebrations surrounding his success, Aarav remained grounded in gratitude and humility. He acknowledged the sacrifices and unwavering support of his friends, particularly Rajat and Rohan, who had stood by him through every challenge. Aarav recognized that his achievement was not solely his own but a collective victory stemming from their shared dreams and aspirations from their humble beginnings in Gauravpur to the bustling streets of Mumbai. Sensitive to the undercurrents of envy that Rajat and Rohan wrestled with, Aarav made deliberate efforts to validate their feelings and provide reassurance. He understood that his success had inadvertently stirred feelings of comparison and self-reflection among his friends. Aarav fostered open lines of communication, encouraging Rajat and Rohan to express their thoughts and concerns without fear of judgment. Despite his best intentions, Aarav could not overlook the shifting dynamics within their group. The once seamless camaraderie now navigated uncharted waters, tested by the complexities of jealousy and competition. He grappled with the delicate balance of celebrating his achievement while empathizing with his friends' internal struggles. Aarav's journey to success prompted introspection, prompting him to contemplate the nature of ambition, friendship, and the inevitable conflicts that arise when paths diverge.

The Impact

As envy began to take root, subtle tensions surfaced in their interactions. Rajat's pragmatic approach occasionally clashed with Rohan's emotional responses, creating moments of friction within their tight-knit circle. Conversations that once flowed effortlessly now tiptoed around sensitive topics, as each friend navigated their own insecurities and aspirations. The strain threatened to erode the foundation of trust and understanding they had painstakingly built over years of friendship. Amidst the mounting tension, effective communication became crucial in navigating their evolving dynamics. Aarav initiated heartfelt conversations, encouraging Rajat and Rohan to voice their concerns openly. He listened with empathy, offering reassurance and understanding as they grappled with conflicting emotions. Priya, perceptive and supportive as always, provided a listening ear and a source of strength for Aarav, offering insights that helped him navigate the intricacies of their friendship. The challenges posed by envy became an opportunity for vulnerability and growth within their group. Rajat confronted his feelings of inadequacy with courage, acknowledging the deeper insecurities that fuelled his envy. Rohan embraced moments of introspection, recognizing the importance of authenticity in navigating professional and personal aspirations. Their willingness to confront these challenges together strengthened their bond, fostering a deeper sense of empathy and mutual respect.

Healing Wounds & Reaffirmation of Bonds

Over time, the wounds inflicted by jealousy began to heal, replaced by a renewed sense of solidarity and mutual support. Rajat and Rohan's introspection led to personal growth, enabling them to wholeheartedly celebrate Aarav's success. They found solace in realizing that their journeys, though unique, were interconnected by a shared commitment to friendship and collective aspirations. The reaffirmation of their bonds unfolded through shared experiences and heartfelt conversations.

Aarav, Rajat, Rohan, and Vikram revisited the essence of their friendship, celebrating each other's triumphs and standing united during challenging times. They embraced the complexities of envy and competition as natural facets of their individual paths, forging a stronger bond built on mutual respect and unwavering support.

Chapter 11: The Rift Deepens - Friendship Tested

In the wake of Aarav's remarkable success and the subtle seeds of envy that had begun to take root among Rajat and Rohan, Chapter 11 delves into a tumultuous period where misunderstandings and petty rivalries threatened to unravel the strong bond forged over years of shared dreams and challenges in Mumbai.

The once harmonious dynamic among Aarav, Rajat, Rohan, and Vikram began to show cracks under the weight of jealousy and unspoken tensions. Misunderstandings, fuelled by unaddressed insecurities and growing differences in perspective, slowly drove a wedge between them. What had once been a circle of unwavering support and camaraderie now echoed with the hollow sounds of resentment and unspoken grievances.

The subtle undercurrents of envy, born out of comparison and unfulfilled aspirations, manifested in subtle ways. Rajat, the pragmatic planner of the group, found himself increasingly withdrawn into his thoughts, grappling with the shadow of his own ambitions cast against Aarav's shining success. His pragmatic approach, once a pillar of strength, now masked a simmering discontent that occasionally spilled over into moments of friction within the group.

Rohan, on the other hand, struggled with his vibrant exterior contrasting with the insecurities gnawing at his core. Despite his outward cheerfulness, the success of his friends, particularly Aarav, served as a stark reminder of the uncertainties he harboured about his own career path and achievements. His infectious laughter, which had often been the glue holding their group together, now felt strained under the weight of unspoken doubts and hesitations.

Words Spoken in Anger, Hearts Broken

As tensions simmered beneath the surface, the fragile peace among the friends shattered in moments of heated confrontation. Words, spoken in anger and frustration, pierced through the veil of camaraderie they had once cherished. Rajat, unable to fully contain his feelings of inadequacy, lashed out at Aarav during a discussion about career aspirations, accusing him of overshadowing their dreams with his success.

Rohan, caught between his admiration for Aarav and his own internal struggles, found himself inadvertently siding with Rajat during the argument. His attempts to mediate only escalated the conflict, further deepening the rift that had begun to form among them. Aarav, stunned by the sudden turn of events, struggled to comprehend the depth of his friends' feelings and the impact his success had inadvertently wrought upon their friendship.

The fallout was profound. Hearts once intertwined with trust and mutual respect now lay broken, wounded by the sharp edges of words spoken in haste and unbridled emotions. Each friend retreated into their own thoughts, grappling with the aftermath of the rift that had torn through the fabric of their once unbreakable bond.

On the Brink of Collapse

In the aftermath of the confrontation, the friendship stood at a precarious precipice. The rift deepened, threatening to engulf them in a chasm of irreconcilable differences and wounded pride. Rajat and Rohan, once stalwart pillars of support for each other and Aarav, found themselves questioning the very foundation upon which their friendship had been built.

The once-shared dreams now seemed distant and out of reach, obscured by the shadows of jealousy and misunderstanding. Their circle, once a sanctuary of shared laughter and mutual encouragement, now echoed with the silence of unresolved conflicts and fractured trust. Each friend grappled with feelings of betrayal and remorse, haunted by the realization that their actions had pushed them perilously close to losing what they had cherished most - their bond of friendship.

Chapter 12: Facing the Truth - Confronting Reality

Amidst the chaos and turmoil that had engulfed their once vibrant friendship, Chapter 12 unfolds as a pivotal moment of introspection and reckoning for Rajat and Rohan. Confronted with the harsh reality of their actions and the fractures within their circle, they embark on a journey of self-discovery and reconciliation, seeking to mend the wounds before irreparable damage is done.

A Moment of Clarity

In the midst of emotional turmoil, a moment of clarity dawns upon Rajat and Rohan. They come to realize that their jealousy and resentment were not rooted in malice towards Aarav, but in their own fears and insecurities. The success that had once inspired them now loomed as a daunting shadow, casting doubt upon their own paths and aspirations.

Rajat, the pragmatic planner whose ambitions had often been driven by a desire for success on his own terms, confronted the stark reality that his comparison with Aarav had clouded his judgment. His relentless pursuit of goals had blinded him to the unique journey each of them was meant to tread. His initial feelings of envy towards Aarav's success were overshadowed by a deeper understanding of the value in celebrating each other's achievements, regardless of how they measured against his own.

Rohan, the spirited heart whose infectious energy had been a source of joy for their group, confronted his own vulnerabilities with newfound introspection. He recognized that his insecurities about career choices and achievements had fuelled the unintended rift between them. His admiration for Aarav's success had unwittingly fed into feelings of inadequacy, prompting him to question the authenticity of his own journey and contributions to their friendship. Armed with this newfound clarity, Rajat and Rohan embark on a journey of reconciliation and self-reflection. They acknowledge the wounds inflicted by their words and actions, driven not by ill intent but by a lack of understanding and empathy in the face of their own insecurities. Their journey through Mumbai, once a tapestry woven with shared dreams and aspirations, now becomes a path of healing and renewal as they seek to confront the truth that had eluded them amidst the turmoil.

Redemption Through Understanding

Through heartfelt conversations and moments of vulnerability, Rajat and Rohan begin to rebuild the bridges they had inadvertently burned. They confront the truth that their friendship, forged through years of shared experiences and mutual support, was resilient enough to withstand the storms of jealousy and misunderstanding that had threatened to tear them apart. Their willingness to confront their fears and acknowledge their shortcomings becomes a testament to the strength of their bond and the depth of their commitment to each other's growth and happiness. As Rajat and Rohan navigate the complexities of forgiveness and reconciliation, they emerge with a renewed commitment to their friendship and shared aspirations. They recognize that the road ahead may not always be smooth, fraught as it is with challenges and uncertainties. Yet, armed with a deeper understanding of themselves and each other, they vow to cherish and nurture the bond they had almost lost.

Chapter 13: Soul Searching - Finding Redemption

In Chapter 13, "Soul Searching - Finding Redemption," Rajat and Rohan embark on a profound journey of introspection and self-discovery, grappling with regret and seeking solace amidst the fractured remains of their once unbreakable friendship. This chapter explores their individual paths towards redemption, delving deep into their hearts and confronting the fears and insecurities that had driven them apart.

Haunted by Regret and Remorse

Following their heated confrontation with Aarav, Rajat and Rohan found themselves haunted by profound regret and remorse. The wounds inflicted by their words ran deep, challenging the very foundation of their friendship. Each reflected on their actions, wrestling with the consequences and the underlying emotions that had led to such a rupture. Rajat, known for his pragmatic approach, had always envisioned success on his own terms. However, Aarav's recent achievement triggered a wave of complex emotions within him. While he genuinely celebrated Aarav's success, envy and self-doubt gnawed at him beneath the surface. His introspective journey took him back's to the dreams they had nurtured since their days in Gauravpur, where ambition and camaraderie had once intertwined seamlessly. Rajat sought solace in those memories, realizing how far they had strayed amidst the pressures of their careers. He confronted his own insecurities, grappling with the contrast between his aspirations and the path he had chosen.

Rohan's Journey: Embracing Vulnerability and Authenticity

Rohan, the spirited heart of their circle, faced a different kind of internal battle. His infectious energy and enthusiasm had often masked deep-seated insecurities. Aarav's success, which he genuinely admired, inadvertently stirred feelings of inadequacy within him. In moments of solitude, Rohan embarked on a journey of self-reflection, revisiting the highs and lows of his career in Mumbai's competitive marketing landscape. He confronted the pressures to succeed and the fear of falling short, acknowledging the shadow that Aarav's success had cast over his own journey. Embracing vulnerability became his strength, as he realized that authenticity was crucial not only in his professional endeavours but also in reclaiming the integrity of their friendship.

Seeking Solace in Memories and Shared Dreams

Together and separately, Rajat and Rohan sought solace in the memories of their friendship and the dreams they had once shared. They revisited old haunts where their youthful dreams had taken root, reminiscing about the bonds that had shaped their journey through life's uncertainties. In these moments of reflection, they found clarity amidst the turmoil, realizing that their friendship was worth fighting for, despite the challenges that lay ahead.

Chapter 14: The Road to Redemption - Struggling to Rise

Chapter 14, "The Road to Redemption - Struggling to Rise," chronicles Rajat and Rohan's journey towards reclaiming their lost dreams with newfound determination and unwavering resolve. This chapter explores their individual paths to self-discovery as they confront every obstacle and challenge that stands between them and their aspirations. Armed with newfound clarity and a renewed sense of purpose, Rajat and Rohan set out on a journey of personal and professional growth. They acknowledged the wounds inflicted by their actions and the rift that had tested their friendship, but they were determined not to let it define their future. Each day became a testament to their resilience and commitment to rise above the shadows of their past misunderstandings.

Rajat's Pursuit of Success

For Rajat, the journey towards redemption meant realigning his ambitions with a deeper sense of purpose and humility. He channelled his pragmatic approach into revaluating his career goals, recognizing the importance of authenticity and integrity in his professional pursuits. Seeking mentorship from experienced entrepreneurs and industry leaders, Rajat drew inspiration from their journeys of resilience and perseverance. His entrepreneurial ventures, once driven by a desire for individual success, now embraced a collaborative spirit rooted in the values of teamwork and mutual respect. Rajat's efforts to rebuild trust within their circle were met with cautious optimism as he navigated the complexities of forgiveness and earned back the respect he had inadvertently jeopardized. Meanwhile, Rohan's journey towards redemption led him to embrace vulnerability as a strength rather than a weakness. He immersed himself in creative endeavours and marketing campaigns that resonated with authenticity and innovation. Seeking mentorship from seasoned marketers and industry experts, Rohan refined his skills and reclaimed his passion for storytelling through digital media. His journey was marked by moments of self-discovery and personal growth as he confronted the insecurities that had once clouded his judgment. Rohan's willingness to acknowledge his vulnerabilities endeared him to his colleagues and peers, fostering camaraderie and mutual support within their professional network. As Rajat and Rohan navigated the road to redemption, they encountered obstacles that tested their resolve and resilience. The pressures of competition and the complexities of rebuilding trust within their circle pushed them to confront their fears head-on. Each setback became a stepping stone towards personal growth and self-discovery, reinforcing their determination to rise above the shadows of their past mistakes. In their respective careers, Rajat and Rohan faced professional challenges that demanded innovation and adaptability. Rajat's entrepreneurial ventures thrived under his renewed focus on collaboration and ethical business practices. He forged partnerships with like-minded individuals and organizations, leveraging their collective strengths to create sustainable solutions that resonated with their shared values. Meanwhile, Rohan's journey through Mumbai's dynamic marketing landscape inspired him to embrace creativity and authenticity in his campaigns. Collaborating with diverse teams and industry influencers, Rohan explored new avenues for storytelling and digital engagement. His resilience in the face of adversity earned him the respect and admiration of his peers as he continued to redefine success on his own terms.

Chapter 15: Aarav's Sacrifice - A Friend in Need

The Beacon of Hope

Despite the rift that had formed between them, Aarav remained a beacon of hope for Rajat and Rohan. His selflessness and compassion served as a guiding light, inspiring them to keep fighting for their dreams, no matter the odds. Aarav's unwavering support was rooted in a deep-seated belief in their potential and a commitment to their collective journey of growth and self-discovery. Throughout their tumultuous journey, Aarav offered guidance and encouragement to Rajat and Rohan with humility and empathy. He listened to their concerns and fears, providing a listening ear and a source of strength during moments of doubt. Aarav's ability to navigate the complexities of their friendship with grace and understanding reinforced their shared commitment to forgiveness and reconciliation. As Rajat and Rohan confronted their own insecurities and ambitions, Aarav's sacrifices became a poignant reminder of the true essence of friendship. His willingness to set aside personal pride and ego in favour of supporting his friends underscored the depth of his character and the strength of their bond. Aarav's sacrifices were not just acts of kindness but reflections of the values they had once shared as aspiring young men in Gauravpur. Aarav's sacrifices inspired Rajat and Rohan to rise above their own shortcomings and embrace the journey towards redemption with renewed vigour. His presence became a source of motivation and courage as they confronted the obstacles that stood between them and their aspirations. Rajat and Rohan drew strength from Aarav's unwavering belief in their potential, forging ahead with determination and resilience.

Chapter 16: The Power of Forgiveness - Reconciliation

The passage of time has a way of soothing the most profound wounds, offering the balm of perspective and the solace of distance. As the days turned into weeks and then months, the friends, once inseparable, began to feel the pangs of absence keenly. What was once a tight-knit circle had splintered, and in those fragments, each individual found themselves grappling with their own regrets and reflections.

Rachel, the most outspoken of the group, often found herself staring out of her apartment window, lost in thought. The skyline seemed to mirror her emotions— vast, beautiful, but often obscured by clouds. She missed the laughter, the shared secrets, the feeling of belonging. She realized that her stubbornness and refusal to listen had been a significant part of the problem. Her heart ached for the camaraderie they had lost.

Tom, the quiet thinker, had always been the glue that held them together. His gentle nature and wise counsel had diffused many a tense situation. But in the aftermath of their fallout, he felt like he had failed his friends. He spent many nights tossing and turning, replaying their arguments and wondering what he could have done differently. Slowly, he began to understand that sometimes, it wasn't about fixing others but allowing them to find their own way to the truth.

Sarah, with her empathetic nature, was perhaps the most affected. She had always been the emotional anchor, the one who sensed the undercurrents of feelings even before they surfaced. The discord among her friends left her feeling unmoored. In her solitude, she began to write letters—letters she never intended to send. They were letters of apology, of explanation, of love. Through her words, she began to forgive herself and, in turn, forgive her friends.

David, ever the pragmatic, initially buried himself in work, hoping that productivity would mask his loneliness. But success tasted hollow without anyone to share it with. The silence in his apartment grew louder, echoing with memories of shared meals, late-night discussions, and collective dreams. He began to recognize the futility of holding onto grudges and the strength it took to forgive.

Forgiveness is often misunderstood as a single act of saying "I forgive you." In reality, it is a process—a journey that involves acknowledging pain, understanding the reasons behind it, and choosing to let go. For these friends, it was no different. Each of them walked this path in their own time, in their own way.

Rachel decided to take the first step. She reached out to Tom, the one she had always felt most comfortable with. It was a simple text: "Can we talk?" The response was immediate and affirmative. They met at their favourite coffee shop, a place that held countless memories of happier times.

Sitting across from each other, the silence was initially awkward, laden with the weight of unspoken words. Rachel took a deep breath and began, "Tom, I know I've been difficult. I let my pride get in the way, and I'm sorry."

Tom's eyes softened. "Rachel, we all had our moments. I should have been more proactive in addressing our issues. I missed you."

As they talked, the barriers began to crumble. They laughed about old times, shared their individual journeys of introspection, and found common ground in their desire to rebuild what was broken. This initial step paved the way for further reconciliation.

Sarah, emboldened by Rachel's courage, decided to call David. Her heart pounded as she dialled his number, half-expecting him not to answer. But he did. "David, it's Sarah. Can we meet?"

David was hesitant but agreed. They met at a park, a neutral ground where they had spent many afternoons talking about everything under the sun. The conversation was stilted at first, but as they walked, the familiar rhythm of their friendship began to re-emerge.

"David, I've written so many letters to you all. I never sent them because I didn't know if you'd want to hear from me," Sarah confessed.

David stopped walking and looked at her, "I wish you had. I've missed your presence, Sarah. Your empathy was always our guiding light."

Their conversation meandered through their past hurts and misunderstandings, but ultimately, it led them back to the essence of their friendship. They hugged, tears streaming down their faces, each tear a testament to the pain they were ready to leave behind.

The final step was bringing everyone together. It was Rachel who took the initiative, organizing a dinner at her place. She cooked their favourite dishes, ensuring that each meal had a memory attached to it. Tom brought wine, Sarah brought dessert, and David, surprisingly, brought a bouquet of flowers—something he had never done before.

As they sat around the table, the initial awkwardness quickly dissolved into laughter and nostalgia. They reminisced about their college days, their adventures, and even their arguments, now seen through the lens of time as learning experiences rather than points of contention.

Rachel raised her glass, "To forgiveness, to understanding, and to the bond that has always been stronger than our differences."

Tom, Sarah, and David clinked their glasses with hers, each silently vowing to cherish and nurture the friendship they had almost lost.

Chapter 17: Reunion - Coming Together Again

With the bitterness of the past behind them, the friends' reunion was a testament to the resilience of true friendship. Their bond, now fortified by forgiveness and understanding, felt unbreakable. They came together not just to relive old memories but to create new ones, stronger and more meaningful.

The night of their reunion was one of celebration. Rachel's apartment was filled with the aroma of home-cooked food, the air buzzing with excitement and anticipation. The table was set with care, each place setting a reminder of the cherished place each friend held in her heart. There were candles flickering, casting a warm, inviting glow, and soft music playing in the background, setting the perfect ambiance for the evening.

As the doorbell rang, Rachel felt a flutter of nerves. It was Tom, punctual as always, carrying a bottle of their favourite wine. He smiled warmly, the same smile that had always reassured her in the past. "This place looks amazing, Rachel."

"Thank you, Tom. I'm so glad you're here," she replied, embracing him.

Soon after, Sarah arrived, her face lighting up the moment she stepped inside. "It's like stepping back into the past, but better," she said, her eyes shining with unshed tears.

David was the last to arrive, fashionably late but with a bouquet of flowers that took everyone by surprise. "I figured it's never too late to start new traditions," he said with a grin.

They gathered around the table, and as they began to eat, the initial stiffness melted away. The food was delicious, each bite a reminder of the comfort they found in each other's company. They laughed as they recounted old stories, like the time they got lost on a road trip and ended up discovering a hidden gem of a diner, or the infamous Halloween party where David's costume was the talk of the night.

As the night wore on, the conversation deepened. They spoke about their personal journeys during the time they were apart, the lessons they had learned, and how those lessons had shaped them. Rachel shared how she had taken up painting as a way to process her emotions, finding solace in the strokes of her brush. Tom talked about his decision to finally pursue his dream of writing, finding his voice through words. Sarah spoke of her volunteer work, how helping others had helped her heal. David revealed his newfound passion for cooking, a surprising but therapeutic discovery.

They toasted to their growth, to the strength it took to confront their flaws, and to the courage it took to forgive. Each friend expressed their gratitude for the others, acknowledging the unique role each had played in their collective journey. There was a profound sense of appreciation, not just for the good times but for the struggles that had brought them closer together.

Rachel, feeling a wave of emotion, proposed a toast. "To us, to our friendship, and to the power of forgiveness. May we always find our way back to each other, no matter what."

They clinked their glasses, the sound a harmonious echo of their renewed bond. The night was filled with joy and a renewed sense of connection, a celebration of the love and loyalty that had withstood the test of time.

In the days that followed, the friends made a conscious effort to stay connected. They planned regular get-togethers, ensuring that their bond remained strong. They supported each other's endeavours, celebrating successes and offering comfort during challenges. The scars of the past had not vanished, but they had become part of the tapestry of their friendship, a testament to their resilience and capacity for forgiveness.

The reunion marked the beginning of a new chapter in their lives. They understood that true friendship was not about the absence of conflict but about the willingness to work through it, to forgive, and to grow together. They had emerged from their trials stronger, their bond deeper and more meaningful.

As they moved forward, they carried with them the lessons they had learned. They knew that there would be more challenges ahead, but they faced the future with confidence, knowing that they had each other to lean on. Their friendship, once tested, had proven to be unbreakable, a source of strength and joy in their lives.

Chapter 18: Dreams Rekindled - A New Beginning

With their friendship restored, Aarav, Rajat, Rohan, and Vikram felt an invigorating sense of purpose and unity. Each of them, despite their unique aspirations and personalities, shared a common goal: to embrace the future with open hearts and determined spirits, ensuring that they pursued their dreams together.

Aarav, the creative mind of the group, had always dreamt of starting his own advertising agency. His vision was clear—a company that didn't just create advertisements but told stories that resonated with people. The rift among his friends had put a temporary halt to his plans, but with the reconciliation, he felt a renewed sense of confidence. He approached his friends with the idea, hoping they would support his endeavour.

Rajat, ever the strategist, saw the potential in Aarav's idea. He had a knack for numbers and business development, skills that perfectly complemented Aarav's creativity. "We can make this happen, Aarav," he said, his eyes gleaming with excitement. "We just need a solid business plan, some initial funding, and of course, our combined effort."

Rohan, the tech-savvy member of the group, immediately began brainstorming ways to leverage digital platforms to boost their prospective business. "We live in a digital age. If we can create a strong online presence and use social media effectively, we can reach a wider audience without significant upfront costs."

Vikram, the empathetic and people-oriented one, knew his role would be to manage the human resources side of the business. He had always been good at understanding people, at bringing out the best in them. "We need to build a team that shares our vision and passion. If we can create a positive work culture, our employees will give their best, and our clients will feel the difference."

With their roles defined, the friends began to lay the groundwork for their venture. They spent countless nights in Aarav's living room, turning it into a makeshift office. There were whiteboards filled with ideas, business models, and timelines. The excitement was palpable as they discussed their strategies, laughed over their silly mistakes, and motivated each other through moments of doubt.

The initial days were tough. They faced rejections from potential investors, struggled with budget constraints, and had to juggle their current jobs to keep the dream afloat. But every setback was met with collective resilience. They brainstormed solutions, adapted their strategies, and kept pushing forward, driven by the shared belief that they were building something significant together.

Their first breakthrough came from an unexpected quarter. A small local business, impressed by their pitch and passion, decided to take a chance on them. It was a modest project, but it meant the world to the friends. They poured their hearts into the campaign, ensuring every detail was perfect. The hard work paid off, and the campaign was a success, earning them accolades and more importantly, confidence.

As word of their creative prowess spread, more clients began to take notice. They started landing bigger projects, and their small venture began to grow. Each success was a testament to their teamwork, and each challenge they overcame only strengthened their bond. They celebrated every milestone, big or small, always taking a moment to appreciate how far they had come.

Aarav's vision of a storytelling-driven agency began to take shape. Rajat's business acumen ensured their growth was sustainable, while Rohan's digital expertise helped them carve a niche in the competitive market. Vikram's people skills fostered a work environment where creativity thrived, and employees felt valued.

Amidst the hectic pace of building a business, they never lost sight of their friendship. They made it a point to take breaks, to unwind and reconnect outside the professional sphere. Whether it was a weekend getaway, a movie night, or just a casual dinner, these moments kept their bond strong and reminded them of the importance of balance.

Their journey was far from over, but as they looked at the flourishing business they had built together, they felt a profound sense of achievement. They had not only rekindled their dreams but had also created a tangible testament to their friendship. The road ahead was still fraught with challenges, but they faced it with courage and determination, knowing that as long as they had each other, they could overcome anything.

Chapter 19: Celebrating Life - Embracing Joy

The friends decided to take a well-deserved break to celebrate their journey so far. Amidst the chaos of life and the relentless pursuit of their dreams, they recognized the need to pause, reflect, and revel in the joy of their achievements and the strength of their bond.

They planned a trip to a serene hillside retreat, a place where they could disconnect from the world and reconnect with each other. As they drove up the winding roads, the fresh air and scenic beauty filled them with a sense of peace and anticipation. The retreat was a charming, rustic cabin surrounded by lush greenery and a clear, starry sky.

The first night, they gathered around a bonfire, the flames dancing in the cool night breeze. The crackling fire and the distant sounds of the forest created a magical ambiance. Aarav, always the storyteller, began recounting their journey, from the early days of their friendship to the recent challenges they had overcome. His words were met with nods of agreement, laughter, and moments of reflective silence.

They toasted to their friendship, each clinking of glasses symbolizing a shared memory, a shared dream. As the night grew deeper, they found themselves dancing beneath the stars. There was no music, just the natural rhythm of their laughter and the bond they shared. It was a moment of pure, unadulterated joy, a celebration of life and the journey they had undertaken together.

Rajat, usually the reserved one, let his guard down, sharing stories and jokes that had everyone in splits. Rohan, the tech wizard, tried to capture the moment on his phone, but eventually, he put it away, realizing that some moments are best lived fully rather than through a lens. Vikram, with his natural charm, pulled everyone into a group hug, emphasizing the love and camaraderie they shared.

The following days were filled with activities that brought them even closer. They hiked through the woods, exploring trails and discovering hidden waterfalls. Each step was a reminder of the journey they were on, each discovery a metaphor for the new experiences they were embracing together. They cooked meals together, their laughter and banter making even the simplest tasks enjoyable.

One evening, they decided to have a talent show, each showcasing a hidden skill. Aarav painted a beautiful landscape, capturing the essence of their surroundings. Rajat surprised everyone with his guitar skills, strumming tunes that had them all singing along. Rohan, ever the tech enthusiast, created a short video montage of their journey, a visual diary that brought tears to their eyes. Vikram, with his soulful voice, sang a song that perfectly encapsulated their friendship.

These moments of joy and togetherness were not just a break from their hectic lives but a reaffirmation of their bond. They realized that amidst the pursuit of success, it was these simple, shared moments that truly enriched their lives. The retreat was a reminder to celebrate life, to embrace joy, and to cherish the relationships that made their journey worthwhile.

As they packed up to leave the retreat, there was a sense of renewal among them. They were ready to face the challenges ahead, but this time with a deeper understanding of what truly mattered. They had found a balance between ambition and contentment, between striving for success and appreciating the present.

Back in the city, they returned to their routine with a renewed sense of purpose. Their business continued to grow, but they never let it overshadow their friendship. They instituted regular breaks, ensuring that they took time to celebrate their achievements and recharge. These moments of pause and reflection became a vital part of their journey, a way to stay grounded and connected.

Their clients and employees began to notice the unique energy in their company. It wasn't just about the creative work they produced but the genuine camaraderie and joy that permeated everything they did. This positive environment attracted more talent, more clients, and more opportunities, creating a virtuous cycle of success and happiness.

As the friends looked back on their journey, they felt a profound sense of gratitude. They had not only rekindled their dreams but had also learned the importance of celebrating life and embracing joy. Their bond, tested by time and trials, had emerged stronger and more resilient. They knew that no matter what the future held, they had each other to lean on, to laugh with, and to celebrate the beautiful journey of life.

Chapter 20: Forever Friends - A Happy Ending

As the sun began to set on the horizon, casting its golden rays upon the world below, the four friends stood hand in hand, their hearts filled with gratitude and love. The journey they had undertaken together was nothing short of extraordinary, a testament to the enduring power of friendship and the unwavering strength of their bond.

The setting sun painted the sky in hues of orange and pink, creating a breathtaking backdrop for their moment of reflection. They stood on a hill overlooking the city, a place they often came to when they needed to think or simply enjoy each other's company. The view was a perfect metaphor for their journey—beautiful, expansive, and filled with promise.

Aarav looked at his friends, his eyes moist with emotion. "We've come a long way, haven't we? From college dreams to building a business, and most importantly, rebuilding our friendship. I can't imagine doing this with anyone else."

Rajat, ever the pragmatist, nodded. "It's been quite a ride. We've had our ups and downs, but we've always found a way back to each other. That's what matters."

Rohan, with his tech-savvy mind and creative spirit, added, "We've built something amazing together, not just a business but a legacy of friendship and trust

"In the tapestry of life, it's the threads of friendship that give it color and strength, weaving a story of love, resilience, and enduring joy."

\-   RAZA KHATIB